T5-AFL-702

1-2

# Junkyard Dan

## Gun in the Back

MEMORIAL LIBRARY
500 N. DUNTON
ARLINGTON HEIGHTS, IL 60004

# NOX PRESS

**books for that extra kick to give you more power**

**www.NoxPress.com**

*Also by Elise Leonard:*

## The **JUNKYARD DAN** series: (*Nox Press*)
1. Start of a New Dan
2. Dried Blood
3. Stolen?
4. Gun in the Back
5. Plans
6. Money for Nothing
7. Stuffed Animal
8. Poison, Anyone?
9. A Picture Tells a Thousand Dollars
10. Wrapped Up
11. Finished
12. Bloody Knife
13. Taking Names and Kicking Assets
14. Mercy

## **THE SMITH BROTHERS** (a series): (*Nox Press*)
1. All for One     5. Master Plan
2. When in Rome
3. Get a Clue
4. The Hard Way

## **A LEEG OF HIS OWN** (a series): (*Nox Press*)
1. Croaking Bullfrogs, Hidden Robbers
2. 20,000 LEEGS Under the C
3. Failure to Lunch
4. Hamlette

## The **AL'S WORLD** series: (*Simon & Schuster*)
Book 1: Monday Morning Blitz
Book 2: Killer Lunch Lady
Book 3: Scared Stiff
Book 4: Monkey Business

# Junkyard Dan

## Gun in the Back

**Elise Leonard**

# NOX PRESS

**books for that extra kick to give you more power**

**www.NoxPress.com**

Leonard, Elise
Junkyard Dan series / Gun in the Back
ISBN: 978-0-9815694-3-7

Copyright © 2008 by Elise Leonard.
All rights reserved, including the right of reproduction in
whole or in part in any form. Published by Nox Press.
www.NoxPress.com

Printed in the U.S.A.
First Nox Press printing: March 2008
Second Nox Press printing: December 2008
Third Nox Press printing: December 2009

**NOX PRESS**
books for that extra kick to give you more power

As always, for my readers, my family
and my friends—old *and* new.

♥ *You guys are the BEST!* ♥

Special thanks to John Formichella
for letting me use a picture of his cool
1930 Ford 5-Window Coupe
on the front cover.

Thanks John!

I hope to catch you and your lovely wife
at a car show soon,
so we can all exchange hugs!
(And that goes for your brother Frank, too!)
☺

And lastly, although there *was* a real Bill McCoy
(of whom the phrase "the real McCoy" *did* originate),
his representation in this book is purely fictional
and does not necessarily represent true events.

*~Elise*

# Chapter 1

"I need some R&R," I said out loud.

Bubba shoveled some of Hilda's pie into his mouth.

"R&R," he said. "What *does* that stand for? Officially."

"Rest and relaxation," I said.

"No," Miles said as he shook his head. "I think it stands for rest and recuperation."

"It does?" Hilda piped in. "I thought it stood for rest and recreation."

"I'm not sure," some guy said. He was sitting at the counter. I think he was a trucker.

He was just passing through. We had no idea who he was.

But that's how things were at Hilda's diner. Everyone was welcome. And everyone spoke to everyone else.

I took a deep breath and let it out slowly. "Yes, well, whatever R&R stands for? I'm not getting *any* of it! Not rest. Not relaxation. Not recuperation. And not *recreation*!"

I guess I was a little tightly wound. By the end of my voiced listing of all the things I wasn't getting? I ended up shouting.

"Man, you're crabby, Dan!" Bubba said.

Bubba was wearing that grin of his. The one that my old Aunt Sue would call "devilish."

"If you'd ask me?" he went on. "It seems like you're not getting a *lot* of things!"

The roar of laughter echoed off the diner's walls.

"I'm glad I can humor everyone," I said.

"*You* don't humor us," Miles said.

"Yeah. It's your *life* that humors us," Bubba explained.

"No offense, buddy. But you don't seem that

funny." That remark came from the trucker at the counter.

"Anyone *else* care to make a crack about my life?" I asked.

I was trying not to smile.

"I *would*," Hilda said. "But you're a big tipper. So it wouldn't be too smart of me."

I nodded. "I'm just glad my pathetic life gives you pleasure."

Then I looked around the diner. My eyes fell to the trucker at the counter.

"Including you," I said.

He smiled over his cup of coffee.

"It sure doesn't seem to be giving *you* any pleasure!" he said.

"Not at the moment," I told him.

"Hey," Bubba said. "You have to admit, Dan. It must feel good to do what you've been doing lately."

"Yeah," Hilda agreed. "All those families you've helped out?"

"Yes," I admitted. "I guess it feels good."

"So far? It's all seemed to work out well," Miles said.

"Mostly because I *made* it work out well," I said gruffly. "But it's been a pain in my butt."

"You've done nice things," Hilda said. "In fact. Here's more pie. Just for being a good guy!"

She placed another slice of pie before me. It had vanilla ice cream on top too. Just the way I liked it.

"Thanks, Hilda," I said with a big smile.

"It's on the house, too," she said.

"Thanks!" I said.

"Is mine on the house?" Bubba asked Hilda.

"No," Hilda said quickly.

Bubba made a face, and we all laughed.

"Speaking of pains in the butt. What about that machine gun?" Bubba asked.

"What about it?" I asked.

"What are you going to *do* about it?" he asked.

"Why do I have to do *anything* about it?!" I bellowed.

"You should, you know," Miles said quietly.

"What part of 'I need some R&R' are you people not *getting*?!" I yelled.

I didn't mean it to be funny. But everyone was laughing.

Hysterically.

## Chapter 2

"I've got it back at the garage," Bubba said.

"So keep it there!" I told him.

"It's *your* machine gun," he said back.

That got the trucker's interest.

"Mr. Goody-Two-Shoes has a machine gun?" he asked.

"No I *don't* have a machine gun!" I responded with a huff.

"Yes you do," Bubba said.

"No I don't," I said back.

"Yes you do," Miles said.

"No I don't," I repeated.

I realized I was acting like a five year old. But I'm sorry. I didn't want that machine gun.

If I *took* the machine gun? Then I had to *do* something *about* it. And I *really* didn't want to.

I'd done enough lately!

"Come on, Bubba," I said. "*You* keep it."

"I don't want it," Bubba said.

"Please?" I asked.

"No," Bubba said firmly. "It's *your* machine gun."

I looked at Miles.

"Don't look at me," Miles said.

I wasn't too proud to beg. I *really* needed a little rest. And peace. And quiet.

"Please?" I begged Miles.

"No," he said firmly. "It's *your* machine gun."

"I'll take it," the trucker said.

"NO!" Bubba, Miles, Hilda and I said together.

The trucker looked at me.

"Where did you get it?" he asked me.

I looked at Bubba.

He snorted a laugh.

"Believe it or not? A little kid found it," Bubba said.

"Found it?!" the trucker asked with disbelief.

"Yeah. He found it wedged in the back of an old 1930 Ford Coupe in Dan's yard," Bubba explained.

"It must have been in a hiding spot. Probably rusted through," Miles said.

I looked at Bubba. "A rusty old car is *not* the place for a child to play!"

"How was *I* supposed to know there was a gun in there?" Bubba asked.

"A rusty car can be dangerous for a child. With*out* the added danger of finding a gun!" I explained.

"His father was there. They couldn't sue you or anything," Bubba whined.

"Want to bet?! Yes! They *could*!" I roared.

I already had someone take every penny that she knew of from me. I didn't need someone *else* taking the pennies she *didn't* take!

"Look. If someone comes with a little kid? And I'm not there? Don't let them use the yard like a jungle gym! Okay? That's all I'm saying," I said to Bubba.

I was sure Miles already knew that.

"Okay," Bubba said. "No problem."

I nodded and finished my pie.

"Why don't you want it?" the trucker asked me.

"Excuse me?" I replied.

"Why don't you want the machine gun?" he asked me.

What kind of question was that?!

"Why don't I want a *machine gun*?" I repeated.

"Yeah," he said.

"Well, first of all. I don't *need* one," I said.

I looked at Bubba.

"He really doesn't," Bubba said.

That was a big help.

"And secondly. If I *take* the gun? I know I'm going to have to track it down. Find out who owned it. And find out why he *had* a gun. Stuff like that. And I've done enough 'tracking things down' lately," I added.

"He really has," Hilda agreed.

The trucker took it all in.

Then he said, "Aren't you curious about it?"

"No," I said simply.

"I am," Bubba said.

"Then *you* find out about it," I said.

"It's *your* gun!" he countered.

I took a deep breath and let it out slowly.

I knew what was going to happen next.

I could feel it in my bones.

I might as well give in now.

I didn't have the energy to fight about it anyhow.

"All right!" I said. "I'll look into it. But can I at least not start until tomorrow?"

Bubba had that twinkle in his eye. "That's okay with me," he said.

"That's fine with me, boss," Miles added.

"Would you *please* stop calling me boss?!" I said to Miles.

"If that's what you want, boss," he said with a grin.

At least when I turn the machine gun in to the sheriff's office? I'll know the story behind it.

## Chapter 3

I played with the dogs for a while. Played catch until I couldn't take it anymore. I even went for a walk with them.

I jogged every now and then. Just to get a little exercise. But every time I jogged? I'd get tripped up by a dog. Or a slime-covered ball.

But at least I'd tried.

I came back and did a little paperwork.

That '69 Camaro I'd sold? I had to file the info on it.

I thought of Roger Strands and his son. Then I smiled.

Restoring the car to its original beauty? Spending time together? They'll have those memories the rest of their lives.

I also smiled at the memory of Doris. Doris Schlumpnuts. She was a real sweetheart.

Now that I had the Camaro's VIN number? My paperwork was done.

So I started to look through the junkyard's files. I wanted to find files or notes on the 1930 Ford Coupe. Of course I found nothing.

That would be too easy!

"I'll have to track it down the hard way," I said out loud.

The cats gave me a dirty look. They didn't like it when I talked to myself. It woke them up.

It must be hard eating and sleeping all day!

I'd have to try it sometime.

But not tomorrow.

Tomorrow, I'd put a call in to Judge Simpkins.

Maybe he could help me.

I got up and went into the back rooms. I got a snack and sat down to watch a little TV.


I must've fallen asleep on the couch. Because

when I woke up? The sun was out.

I woke up with a crick in my neck.

I took a hot shower. But that didn't help any.

Great. I was starting my pain-in-the-neck day with a pain in my neck!

I got dressed in jeans and a t-shirt. Then padded to my little kitchen.

I made a fried egg sandwich. I put it on English muffins.

It was so good, I made myself another.

The cats started to yowl.

"Yes," I told them. "I'm coming to feed you. Give me five minutes."

The dogs heard my voice and started to bark. They wanted to let me know that *they* were hungry too.

"I hear you, guys," I called to them. "I'll be right out."

I got everyone fed. Now it was time to start my day.

I called Judge Simpkins's office.

"Oh. Hi, Dan. Judge Simpkins is out fishing

again," his secretary said.

"Same place?" I asked.

"Same place," she said with a giggle.

"Okay, I'll get my canoe out," I told her.

"All righty then," she said. "Have a nice day!"

I hung up. Then I went to the shed with the truck and canoe.

This was a strange life I was now living.

Meetings in canoes with judges. Old men holding guns to my head. Finding runaway kids.

When I was a stockbroker? I hadn't done anything at *all* like that.

## Chapter 4

I was headed down the river.

I saw another canoe. But it wasn't Judge Simpkins.

I said hello as I passed. But the guy was catching a fish at the time.

I don't think he heard me. I don't think he cared.

I moved downstream.

The next guy I ran into? Judge Simpkins.

He was standing *in* the river.

"Hey there, Dan," he called to me.

He took off his hat and waved it.

The sun beamed off the top of his head. I was glad I wore my shades.

"Hi, Judge," I called back.

He waited for me to glide near him.

"How goes things, son?" he asked.

"Good, thanks," I replied.

"Bubba told me abut the Honda Civic case," he said.

It was funny that he'd used the word "case."

I hadn't thought of it as a "case." But I guess it *was*.

"Heard you also had another case. An old '69 Camaro," he said.

"Yes, sir," I said.

"Heard you solved that case, too."

Hm. I'd never thought of things in that way. But, in a way, I *had* solved that "case."

"Bubba sure does like to talk a lot," I said with a grin.

"Aw. He's just proud of you. Proud to be your friend," Judge Simpkins said.

I got embarrassed.

"No need to get all flustered, son," he said kindly. "I knew you were a good man the first time I met you."

That made me even *more* embarrassed.

I didn't know what to say.

"So what can I do you for?" he said with a loud chuckle.

His belly shook with this laughter. Ripples spread across the river.

They started at his body. Then moved outward.

His chins waggled too.

It was hard not to like Judge Simpkins. I wondered how he handled the tough cases. You know the ones.

I'd bet he was fair. Perhaps tough. But fair.

He seemed to have a big heart.

He seemed to have a big *everything*. The man was as round as a beach ball. But he still had a presence about him.

He had the bearing of a man who held power. But it was clear he didn't abuse that power.

If anything, I'd bet he used it for good.

He certainly helped me whenever I needed it.

"I need your help again," I said simply.

He nodded. His chins setting in motion. "That's fine, son. With what?"

"While I was out on the last, ah, case? It seems a child found a gun at my yard."

"A gun?" he asked. "A hunting gun?"

"No," I said. "A machine gun."

"A *machine* gun! How did *that* get there?!"

"It was shoved in the back of an old car," I told him.

"Which one?" he asked.

"A 1930 Ford Coupe."

"There must be a story behind *that*!" he said.

"We think that the gun's hiding spot rusted out," I explained.

"That makes sense."

"So the gun was now exposed. And the child found it."

"That's probably what happened," he said.

"It's only a guess," I said.

He nodded. "But a good one, I'd think."

"So I want to find out about the gun. Trace the car's owners," I told him.

"Did you run a Car Facts report?" he asked.

"I don't think that'll help. The car is from the 1930s."

"Right. Right," he said.

His chins waggled as he nodded.

"Okay," he said. He started reeling in his line. "Let's go to my office."

"I'll meet you there," I said.

## Chapter 5

I paddled back up the river.

This time? When I passed the guy in the canoe? He waved and smiled.

"Sorry about before," he called.

"No problem," I said. "You had a bite."

He laughed.

"This is the only time I get a little peace and quiet. When I'm on the river," he said.

Ah. Peace and quiet. Maybe that's what I have to do! Maybe I just need to grab a rod and leave the yard.

"A little peace and quiet sounds great!" I said.

"I have twins," he said. "They're three."

I held up my hand. "No need to say more."

He laughed.

"I understand wanting peace and quiet," I told him. "And I don't have *any* kids!"

The man laughed and waved goodbye.

By then? I was almost out of earshot anyhow.

I finally got back to the truck.

Funny. But that crick in my neck? Gone!

Paddling must have worked it out.

Either that? Or I was relaxed and it just went away.

Whatever the reason? I was glad it was gone.

Last time I had a crick in my neck? It had lasted for days! About two weeks, really.

Patti had gotten mad at me.

I told her she couldn't buy another car. I'd just *bought* her a car two months earlier.

But she wanted a *different* car. The same car her girlfriend had.

The car I'd bought her two months before? A girlfriend had just gotten *that* car. That's why Patti *had* to have one.

But then *another* friend bought a more

*expensive* car. And Patti had to have *that* car.

I think I made the mistake of telling her she was being too demanding.

I *know* I made the mistake of saying "no."

I ended up on the couch.

That's how I got the last crick in my neck. And that one lasted two weeks.

That's how long I was thrown out of my bedroom.

It all sounds kind of silly to me now. But I guess you had to be there. Patti had this way of tying me into knots.

And in case you're wondering? To prove that I wasn't a total wuss? I didn't buy her that car!

I didn't have to.

Two weeks later? She bought it herself.

She used my credit rating to get the loan. And then forged my signature.

Now? When I think about things like this? It makes me wonder what I saw in her.

It must be true what they say. Love is blind.

I now know that I was totally blind.

Blinded by love.

I made a mental note to myself. A promise.

"Don't do that ever again, Dan!" I told myself.

Then I smiled.

"Don't worry," I answered myself. "I won't!"

I got out of the canoe. Hitched it up the riverbank. Threw it overhead. Walked the fifty feet to my old pickup. Then swung it into the back of the truck.

I sighed with pleasure.

I was glad the crick in my neck was gone.

Yup. Life was good here. Life sure was good.

I just wish all these problems would stop popping up.

They had to end sooner or later. Right?

Hopefully? It was sooner than later.

With that thought, I got into my truck and headed back to the yard.

## Chapter 6

I pulled the truck into the shed.

Then I ran to my car and hopped in.

The dogs ran after me.

"I can't play now, guys. Sorry. I'll play with you when I get home. Okay?"

They seemed to be okay with that.

I raced down to the courthouse. Then ran to Judge Simpkins's office.

"Go on in, Dan. He's waiting for you," the secretary said.

I went into his office. "You beat me here again," I said with a smile.

He was sitting behind his desk.

"I live a lot closer to where I fish than you do,"

he said.

He was smiling widely. Like he had a secret.

"You have to paddle upstream. Then you have to load up your truck. Then drive home. Then change cars," he said. "*I* just have to get to the riverbank. And hop in my car."

Oh. Right. I forgot. He lives right *on* the river.

"And I live closer to town, too," he said.

He smiled at me.

"Plus, I cheated a little," he added.

Then he chuckled.

"After I help you? I have plans to go back." He got up from behind his desk.

He was still wearing his waders.

I had to laugh.

The man was a character. A *likable* character. But a character.

I think everyone *in* this town was a character.

Take Bubba. A pierced, tattooed, spike-haired, Goth-looking garage mechanic who wears black leather spiked collars and wristbands? He was not what one would expect from a mechanic.

I heard the town librarian was a biker dude named Henry.

I hadn't had time to get to the library yet. But as soon as I did? I had to meet *that* guy!

Hilda says he's really nice.

And speaking of Hilda? She was one of a kind, too! They sure didn't make many women like Hilda.

She was kind, sweet and had a heart of gold. And boy could that woman *cook*!

"So. Let's try calling my friend again," Judge Simpkins said.

I was lost in thought. Thinking about the great people who lived here. So I jumped a little.

"Oh. Right. Sure," I replied.

Judge Simpkins chuckled.

"Having a little daydream?" he asked.

I smiled. "Just thinking about the people in this town."

"Pretty great. Don't you think?" he asked.

I nodded. "Yes they are."

"And now you're one of them," he said kindly.

I smiled. "I'm lucky."

"So are we," he said. "To have you."

It was nice to be thought well of. Nice to be valued. Valued as a person. And not for just the money you made.

I tried to think if anyone else had ever valued me as a person.

My mom. My dad. But that had been it.

He picked up the phone and dialed.

It must have gone through.

"Hi, honey," he said.

He looked at me and winked.

"Where's the big cheese?" he asked.

He laughed at her answer.

"I know. I know. He's like a stinky cheese on some days."

I could hear laughter coming out of the phone.

"I love that!" Judge Simpkins said. "With liverwurst!"

I heard gagging noises come through the phone.

Liverwurst? That was gross!

I agreed with the girl on the phone.

"Thanks, honey," he said.

Then he put his hand over the phone.

"She's getting him," he said.

I nodded.

"He's in a bad mood today," he added.

I nodded again.

"That could only mean a case is not going well," he stated.

"Oh," I said. I had no idea what else to say.

"He's got a *very* stressful job," Judge Simpkins said.

I knew what *that* was like.

"If he fails? People die," he explained.

Oh my God. I wondered what the man *did* for a living.

## Chapter 7

Judge Simpkins held up his finger. As if to say, "Hang on a minute."

Then he spoke into the phone.

"Hey," he said. "Having a tough day?"

I couldn't hear the reply. The man must speak softly. At least, softer then the woman who answers his phone.

I watched as Judge Simpkins's face dropped.

"Oh that's rough. I'm sorry," he told the man.

He listened some more.

"Maybe I should call back another day," he offered.

He waited for a reply.

"Well, it's about a machine gun," he said.

I could hear the man now. "Get it off the streets!" he boomed.

"It *is* off the streets. Don't worry. My friend Dan. You remember him. Right? He found it in the back of an old 1930 Ford Coupe."

The man was speaking softly again. I couldn't hear his response.

"A child found it, actually," Simpkins told the man.

More muffled response.

"After *your* day? Maybe this should wait," he said.

I could hear the man again. He was saying that he wanted to help.

"Dan has the VIN number," the judge said.

He waved at me to give it to him.

I took it from my wallet. Then I handed it to him.

He read the number to his friend.

"A search would be fine," he said.

He waited.

"No that's great. Really. Thank you! Can I give

you Dan's number?"

The judge winked at me.

"Yes. You can call him at the yard. Don't worry. He doesn't have caller ID at the yard. It's an old land line."

He gave his friend my phone number.

My *business* phone number.

He knew it by heart. But I guess it had been the same number for well over thirty years.

It had been Junkyard Dan's number long before I got there.

I smiled at my next thought.

It was probably one of the first phones in the town!

"Sure thing," Judge Simpkins said into the phone. "Good luck with what you're working on! And thanks again."

He hung up the phone.

He grimaced and shook his head. "That poor guy. He has a hard job!"

"Sounds like it," I said.

"I couldn't do his job," he said.

I wondered what the man did. But I knew better than to ask.

"You know what they say. Right?" he asked.

"No," I said. "What do they say?"

"It's a hard job. But *someone's* got to do it."

All of a sudden? Judge Simpkins looked old and tired.

"You need to get back to the yard. He'll call you there," he said.

"Okay. Will do. Thanks. For everything," I said.

"Any time, Dan. Any time," he replied.

He hefted his body from behind his desk.

"And now? Now I need to get back out on that river," he said.

I didn't know what the man on the phone had said. But *whatever* it was? It sure shook up Judge Simpkins.

I nodded and left.

## Chapter 8

I had no idea how long it would take for him to call. But I rushed back.

I also hung out by the office.

Stayed by the phone.

I didn't want the man to call, and I wasn't there.

I knew from the last time he helped me that I couldn't know his name. Or what he did.

But I sure was curious.

Whatever he'd said to Judge Simpkins? It sure did upset the judge.

I was playing with the dogs. Throwing the ball when the phone rang.

I ran inside to get the phone.

"Hello. This is Dan," I said.

"Hey, Dan," a man said. "This is the judge's friend."

"Hi," I said.

"I ran that VIN," he said. "The results were…"

He paused.

"…very interesting," he finished.

I wondered what that meant.

I wondered if he'd *tell* me.

I wondered if I should ask. I wanted to.

But didn't know if I should.

"It seems that car you have? It was seized. A long, *long* time ago. By the police."

The *police*?!

"It was taken when it was a new car," he said.

"Back in *1930*?" I asked.

"Yup. It was a brand new car. Fresh off the assembly line. Maybe only a few weeks old," he said.

"Why was it seized?" I asked.

"That, I can't tell you," he said. "But I *can* tell you a name."

"The owner of the car?" I asked.

"I can't tell you that either," he said. "Just do a search. Google the name I give you. You'll be able to track down the story, I'm sure."

Oh great. Another goose chase. Just what I need.

There go my hopes of getting some R&R.


I'd written down the name. But to be honest? I was afraid to look it up.

I was afraid of the wasps' nest I'd find myself in.

It seemed that every time I got involved in something? It was another problem. A long, drawn out problem.

I needed less problems in my life. Not more problems.

So I *did* write down the name. But I just folded up the paper. Then I stuck it in my wallet.

Hoping I'd forget about it.

But, of course, I didn't.

It felt like it was burning a hole in my pocket.

I kept my wallet in my back pocket. My left back pocket.

So, I had a burning in my butt.

The left-hand side of my butt.

My left butt cheek, to be exact.

## Chapter 9

I pushed a cat off my computer tower.

"Time to move it, Cat," I said.

The cat looked annoyed. But this one always looked annoyed.

At least I *think* it was this one.

I had a lot of cats. They hung out all over the place. So he may be a new one. Or he may be the one I was thinking about. I couldn't tell.

But usually? Most of them were annoyed with me. At least at one time or another.

He jumped from the tower and landed on the floor. Then he jumped up from the floor. Right into my lap.

Guess he wanted to move from one warm place

to another.

He walked around in a circle. Then he plopped down. He stretched once. Then curled into a ball.

"Comfy?" I asked him.

He opened one eye.

"Comfy?" I asked again.

He purred softly.

Guess that answered my question.

He closed his eye and fell asleep.

I reached over the ball of fur on my lap. I pulled up the Google page.

I typed in the name the guy had given me.

Bert Herpichio.

It was either that or Bert Herpiccio.

He's said there were two spellings. One Italian. The other, an American version.

He told me to look up both.

I tried the Italian way. Bert Herpiccio. But found nothing. Not one listing.

Bert Herpiccio didn't exist. At least not on the Internet.

Then I tried Bert Herpichio. A couple of things

popped up.

Not many. But a couple.

It listed a home address and phone number.

I figured I'd start there.

I didn't know what I'd say to the man.

But figured I'd wing it.

So far I'd been winging it for everything I'd done.

The only time it got me into trouble? Was that time I made the old man's wife cry. Then he stuck a gun to my head.

But he was only protecting his wife. At least he *thought* he was.

He wasn't protecting his wife. I wasn't going to harm anyone! So. Bottom line? He was only scaring the pants off of *me*!

But I got out of that okay.

*This* time? I doubt I'll make this guy cry.

So I didn't have to worry about that.

I looked at the name to get it right.

Bert Herpichio.

I sounded it out. Her *peach* ee oh. With the

accent on the "peach."

I dialed the number on the computer screen.

I got that weird ring tone. You know the one. The one that grates your nerves?

Then a machine voice came on the line.

"We're sorry. The number you are trying to reach has been disconnected. Please check the number. And dial again."

I checked the number. I dialed again.

I got the ring tone.

I got the machine lady.

"We're sorry. The number you are trying to reach has been disconnected. Please check the number. And dial again."

Great. A dead end.

Now I was going to have to dig deeper.

## Chapter 10

I went back to the Google page.

There were three listings.

The first one was the address and phone number.

That was a bust.

The second was about some lawsuit.

I read through it quickly.

It seems he got a hip replaced.

I read some more.

The joint they put in him? It was bad. They had to take it out.

He had to have more surgery. To fix that whole mess.

And not just him.

This happened to hundreds of people!

They were all suing the company that made the part for the hip.

It was a good story. But it didn't help me much.

The third listing? It was a realtor listing.

It was an ad for a house. It listed his name as the owner.

I checked the listing.

I checked the address.

It was the same address as the phone listing I'd just dialed.

But I couldn't give up.

I had no other clues.

I needed to find that man.

So I checked a map. Looked up where his house was.

It was about an hour away.

I figured that maybe he changed his phone number. At least I hoped so.

Maybe he got a cell phone. Maybe he didn't need his land line anymore.

Who knows?

# Gun in the Back

It was worth a try.

I had no other leads.

So I got in my car and went for a drive.


Florida was beautiful. Sunny. Bright. So green.

And all the palm trees? They were cool. Took some getting used to.

But I'd manage.

I drove along the highway at a good pace. Not too fast. Not too slow.

There were other cars on the road. But they stayed in the slow lane. So I could get around them.

I loved driving in this state.

I opened the window and breathed in the fresh air. Took a good lungful.

It smelled salty. I even liked *that*. Fresh salt air.

It seemed so… healthy.

No wonder all the elderly folks moved here. They weren't fools!

And now? I wasn't one either.

As far as warmth? I'd think California was the

same way. And Texas. And Arizona. And Georgia. And New Mexico. And Louisiana. And Mississippi. And Alabama.

Okay. So maybe there were a *lot* of great places to live. New York was a great place to live. But I had to get away from there.

You know. Because of the whole Patti thing.

But this? This I could get used to!

Oh. Who was I fooling! I already *was* used to living here!

I got to Bert's house in an hour. Just like the map page said I would.

But it felt like ten minutes.

I got out of the car. Stretched. Then walked up to the house.

I rang the bell.

I waited.

A little boy answered the door.

"Hi," I said. "Is your mom or dad home?"

"They're deborst. Mommy said that Daddy liked his sexitory too much."

"You mean his secretary?" I asked.

"Yeah. You know her? Daddy calls her Trina. But Mommy calls her Tramp for short. You know. Like a nickname. Like my name is Robert. But Mommy and Daddy call me Bobby. That's not really shorter. But I like it better. Don't you?"

This kid was a talker. Cute. But a real chatterbox.

I didn't want to get him started again.

"Is your mommy home?" I asked him.

"Yeah. She's home. She's shaving the hair off her legs. She's got a date tonight. And she has really hairy legs. She doesn't want the man to know that. So she's shaving them. She doesn't shave her face like Daddy. Oh wait. Sometimes she does. She has a mustache sometimes. But she shaves it off. I think she'll shave that too. Before her date. I heard her friend ask if she was shaving. And Mommy said yeah. Then she said maybe she'll get lucky. Then they both laughed. Are you the man? Will you make Mommy lucky? She's still shaving. She has *very* hairy legs."

## Chapter 11

"Bobby? Was that the door?" a woman called out.

"Yeah," he called back.

"Who was it?" she called.

"My friend," he called back.

"Petie?" she called.

"No," he called back.

"Johnny?" she called.

"No," he called back.

"Mikey?" she called.

"No," he called back.

"Katie?" she called.

"No," he called back.

"Sarah?" she called.

"No," he called back.

"Bobby! Who *was* it?" Her voice was getting shrill.

"A man," he called.

"What did he say?" she called to him.

"Not much," he called.

"Did he leave a *message*?" She was all but shrieking now.

"No," he called.

"Did he leave a *package*?"

"No," he called.

"Did he leave some flowers? *Anything*?"

No," he called. "He was just being my friend."

I heard water splash.

I heard thumping footsteps approach.

"Are you okay?! Do *not* answer the door! *Ever* again! Do you hear me, Bobby? Do *NOT* answer the door!"

A dripping wet woman came storming into view.

She had a towel around her. Barely.

She stopped short when she saw me.

Her mouth opened to scream.

"He's still here, Mommy. Look. This is my friend."

"*Get out*!" she roared. "*Now*!"

For a woman in a towel? Making a puddle where she stood? She sure did have a lot of confidence!

"Whoa. Calm down there," I said gently.

The fact that I'd spoken? It freaked her out *more*.

Her eyes darted to a table. A table with a phone.

It was on the other side of the room.

I saw the moment she made her decision.

She decided to go for it.

She ran toward the phone.

She slipped on the puddle she'd made. She went flying. Feet first.

Head over teakettle.

She must've gotten at least three feet in the air.

It was impressive. Sort of. In a weird way.

She fell with a thud.

Hit hard.

Right on her back.

She knocked the wind out of herself.

Oh yes. And… her towel? It slipped off.

There she was. Lying on the floor. Dripping wet. Hair a knotted mess.

Shaving cream clumped on her legs. Sliding down.

Stark naked.

# Chapter 12

She moaned in pain.

"Are you all right?" I asked.

I took a step.

"*Don't*!" she screamed. "Do *NOT* take one step closer! I'll call the police!"

"Mommy," Bobby said. "You *can't* call the police. You don't have a phone, silly!"

"Bobby," she said. "Get away from that man. Now!"

"But he's my friend," Bobby whined.

The boy looked at me.

"Bobby," I told him. "Do what your mother says."

The boy shrugged. Then he shook his head.

"I think all grownups are loony," he muttered to himself. Not very quietly.

"Get me the phone please, Bobby," the woman said to the boy.

He walked to the phone. Picked it off the cradle. Reached down. And handed it to his mother.

"I'm dialing 911," she said to me.

"Are you hurt?" I asked.

"Stop *looking* at me!" she roared.

I looked away.

"Can I help you?" I asked. "You seem in pain."

I was facing the door.

"Why are you here? What do you want?" she barked at me. "*Leave me and my son alone*!" she screamed.

"I'm just looking for a man," I said.

Before I could explain further? She was yelling again.

"If you're looking for Bruce? He's moved in with that tramp Trina. If you're Trina's boyfriend, husband or father? I give you *full* permission to

*KICK Bruce's…"*

Then she looked at Bobby and stopped talking.

"Well, you know what I give you permission to do," she said weakly.

Yes. I knew.

And if you asked me? "Bruce" deserved what she'd "allowed" me to do.

"Bobby," I said. "Would you please get your mom another towel?"

The boy ran out of the room. Happy to have something to do, I think.

He came back with a washcloth. He handed it to me.

"Have anything a bit *bigger*?" I asked the boy.

"I'll go check," he said. He tore out of the room.

"Look in the linen closet," his mother called to his back.

He called from the other room. "The what?"

"The linen closet. The little door next to the toilet," his mother shouted.

She was lying on the floor. She hadn't moved a

muscle.

I was still trying to look at the door.

Trouble was? I had great peripheral vision. I could see things off to the side really well.

And, I had to admit. No matter *where* I looked? I could see her.

"Bobby?!" she called out. "Where *are* you?"

No answer.

"***Bobby***!" she screamed.

The boy came running back. "That place is *cool*, Mommy! It's like a tiny little room! I didn't even know it was *there*!"

Of course, he had no towel.

"I'll get it," I told the poor woman.

As I headed for the bathroom? I heard a small squeak come out of her.

"Thank you," she squeaked.

## Chapter 13

I felt so sorry for her. That poor woman!

She'd been through a lot lately. Or so it seemed to *me*.

This added event didn't help.

I found the linen closet. I took a bath towel. Then I found a sheet towel.

I grabbed both.

Then I walked back to the entryway. Slowly.

I didn't want to scare her.

"Bobby," I said softly. "Please give these to your mommy."

I didn't want to spook her again. So I kept my voice relaxed and calm.

But the *last* thing I felt? Was relaxed and calm.

Hairy legs and mustache aside? This woman was a knock out!

Even *with* stringy hair. And nervous blotches.

That Bruce guy must be a *complete* moron!

A gorgeous son? A beautiful wife? One who obviously still loved him? Even after all he did to her? He was a *fool*!

How come people don't realize what they have?!

Why are people always looking for greener pastures?

I don't get it sometimes.

This was one of those times.

I heard her snap out the towels. I could see, through my good side vision, that she had them in place.

"Are you okay?" I asked.

"I'm not sure," she said weakly.

"Do you need a doctor?" I asked.

"I don't know," she said.

"Would you like me to call an ambulance?" I asked.

"I can't. I can't leave Bobby. I have no one to watch him," she said softly.

"I'll watch him," I offered.

"*Over my dead body!*" she countered with force.

Wow. This woman was a momma bear if I ever met one!

"I'm not going to hurt your son, Ma'am," I said calmly.

"I don't care. I don't *know* you. I don't *trust* you. I *won't* trust you!"

I think I understood.

Little Bobby was all she had left. She didn't want anything to happen to him. I got that. Loud and clear.

"Okay. Let's just take this a step at a time. All right?" I said gently.

She eyed me warily.

"I guess I have no choice. Do I?!" she uttered.

"I'll call 911," I told her. "We'll get an ambulance here."

"Okay," she said weakly.

## Gun in the Back

The fight was draining out of her.

I just hoped she didn't start crying.

An angry woman? *That* I could deal with.

A *crying* woman?

That's a whole other can of worms!

One I *didn't* want to open!

## Chapter 14

I was afraid that if *this* woman started crying? She'd never stop!

The ambulance came quickly.

The EMT looked her over.

He was a good guy. He never cracked a smile.

I'm sure that was hard to do!

"It seems you've just thrown your back out," he said. "Want me to see if I can pop it back?"

I didn't know if *I'd* go for that.

I wondered if she would.

She was thinking about it.

"*I* want to see that!" Bobby said cheerfully.

Kids. They were funny.

This one was *really* cute.

It made me regret that I didn't have any.

The woman sighed loudly.

"You don't want to miss your date tonight," I said softly.

She blushed. A deep red.

"You *know* about that?" she shrieked.

I nodded and tried not to smile. I failed.

"Bob-*by*!" she wailed.

"He's my *friend*, Mommy," Bobby said in response.

Her eyes flew to me. She didn't look happy.

I couldn't blame her.

"That's all he told me," I said quickly.

Again, I tried not to smile.

Again, I failed.

I was thinking about legs. And mustaches. And tramps. And getting lucky. But with *her* in mind. Not me!

I had no interest in any of that.

Not for now.

Getting burned by Patti? It was too fresh in my head. Too soon to be thinking about any of *that*.

"Okay," she told the EMT guy. "Go ahead. Do your best."

He nodded.

"But don't break my spine or anything!" she warned.

"No, Ma'am. I won't," he said gravely.

She looked at me and grinned crookedly.

What a trooper.

"Okay," the EMT guy said. "Here goes."

"Here goes nothing," she added with another grin.

I saw him scoop her up. He gave her a squeeze.

I heard a pop.

She sighed.

"Ahhh," she said. "That's better. *Much* better!"

"It *worked*?" the EMT guy asked.

He sounded like he couldn't believe it.

She looked at him. "You didn't think it *would*?" she bellowed.

He shrugged and made a face. "I wasn't sure. I just read about it two nights ago. I'm still in training."

At first I thought she was going to yell at him. But then she laughed. And smiled.

Her laughter tinkled. And her smile was radiant. She was a very beautiful woman.

Bruce was an idiot!

## Chapter 15

She was sitting in a chair as the EMT guys packed up.

They were ready to go.

"Anything else I can help you with?" the guy asked her.

"Nope," she said lightly. "You did a great job! Thanks!"

He smiled widely.

Right before he shut the door? She shouted, "Keep studying!"

The door was shut. But we heard him call back, "I will!"

We chuckled at that.

"You're all better, Mommy?" Bobby asked her.

He was stroking her arm. Softly. Like he was trying to take care of her. Make her feel better.

It was sweet.

She scooped him up and plopped him on her lap. "All better, honey! Thank you. You take such *good* care of me."

He jumped off her lap and started running around. In circles.

She looked at me and smiled.

"He does that when he's happy," she said.

He was flying in circles. Going faster and faster.

"He must be *really* happy," I said back.

She smiled.

The look she gave her son was soft and sweet. Full of love.

Then she looked over at me.

"So what can I do for you?" she said. "I can tell you're not the creep, robber or bad guy I'd *thought* you were."

That made me laugh. No. I wasn't any of those things.

"I'm here to speak with Bert. Bert Herpichio. He lives here?"

Maybe he was her father. Or her father in law. Maybe he left when Bruce left. Maybe that's why the phone number was changed.

"He's the man we bought the house from," she said.

"The *former* owner?" I asked.

"Yes," she said.

I made a face. "Dang! Now I'll *never* track him down."

"Is it urgent?" she asked.

I nodded.

"I might have his address," she said as she got up.

Little Bobby was still running in circles.

"Doesn't he get dizzy?" I asked her.

She smiled. "That's the point," she said.

"Yeah," Bobby screamed. "That's the *fun*!"

We walked around his "air field." Gave him plenty of room.

Then I followed her to the kitchen.

She walked to a drawer.

"I think I have the address in here. It's my junk drawer," she said with a smile.

She looked through the drawer.

About a minute later? She pulled out a piece of paper.

"Here it is," she said.

"That's great!" I said.

She handed me the piece of paper.

I looked around to see if there was any pen or paper. So I could copy it.

"Just take it," she said.

"Are you sure?" I asked.

She nodded. "I had to write it on his mail. To forward it," she explained. "It came here for a long time. Not so much any more. Hardly ever."

I nodded.

"Well, thank you for your help," I told her. I shook the piece of paper. "This is what I came for."

She smiled. She had a pretty smile. Beautiful, really.

"No problem," she said.

"And I'm sorry for scaring you," I added.

She nodded shyly. "I tend to go off the deep end lately."

I shrugged. "You've been through a lot."

"Yes, but I should try to stay more calm. For Bobby's sake. If not my own."

She had a point.

I started to head for the front door.

It was time to leave.

Funny, but I didn't want to leave just yet. I had no idea why.

"Good luck on your date tonight," I said to her.

She smiled shyly. "Thanks. He's nothing special. Just someone to make me feel better about myself."

I stopped. I turned. I looked her in the eye.

"Don't get mad at this. Please. But I must tell you. You don't need *anyone* to make you feel better about yourself! You should feel good about yourself for who you are. You're pretty amazing!"

And with that said, I left.

## Chapter 16

I could see her face as I drove off.

She was watching me from the front window. Waving.

I could see tears in her eyes.

I hoped they were tears of joy. Not tears of sorrow.

From what I could tell? She *was* an amazing woman. A good mom. A loving wife.

If it were any other time? I'd ask her out. Get to know her.

But not now. It was too soon after Patti.

Still, I hoped she found happiness.

Hoped she found what she was looking for.

I hoped *I* found what I was looking for too!

And that was… Bert Herpichio.

I looked at the paper.

I looked at my gas gauge.

"I need gas," I said to myself.

I pulled over to get gas.

There was a guy at the same pump. But on the other side.

"Excuse me," I said. "But do you know where this place is?" I asked.

I showed him the paper.

"I think that's a nursing home. About ten miles away. Next town over," he said.

"That sounds about right," I told him. "Thanks."

"Just follow this road for while. Then make a left at the Taco Bell. If it's the one I'm thinking it is? It's on that road."

He looked at the paper again.

"Yeah. That's right. It's on that road anyhow. You can't miss it. Just hang a left at the Taco Bell," he said.

I took the paper back.

"Thanks," I said.

"It'll be on the left," he said.

"Okay. Good. Thanks," I said.

It was easy to find.

Exactly as the guy told me.

I went down the road. I saw Taco Bell. I made a left.

I drove down that road. And it was on my left.

I pulled in and parked.

I got out and walked to the front doors.

It looked like a nice place.

I didn't know what I was expecting. Maybe something gloomy.

But that's not what I found.

This place was great. And it smelled great, too! Food was cooking.

I sniffed the air. Smelled like stew. Beef stew.

There was a lady sitting at the front desk.

"May I help you?" she asked.

"Hi. I'm looking for Bert. Bert Herpichio. Does he live here?"

"He surely does," she said brightly. "Hang on.

I'll get him for you."

She pressed a button on the phone. Then she spoke into it.

"Bert. You have a visitor. Bert you have a visitor. Please come to the front lobby. Bert, please come to the lobby."

I could hear the announcement over the loud speakers.

"Okay," she said brightly. "That ought to do it!"

"Thank you," I said.

"If you'd like? You can sit on one of those chairs. It may be a while," she said.

She was a cheerful little thing.

"Okay," I said.

I headed over to the bank of chairs. I was just about to sit down.

"Did you page me, Jean?" a man asked.

"Sure did, Bert," the cheery woman said.

"I have a *visitor*?" he asked.

"Sure do, Bert," she said with a smile.

She looked at me. "You're his first visitor."

"Today?" I asked.

"Ever," Bert said.

I looked at Jean.

She nodded and grimaced.

From what Bobby's mother said, Bert had been here a long while.

That was kind of sad.

"I don't know who you are. Or why you're here. But I'm glad to see you!" Bert said with feeling. "Thanks for coming!"

He smiled widely.

"Oops," he said. "I ran down here so fast? I forget to put in my teeth!"

"Why don't you take your guest to your room, Bert?" Jean suggested. "That way you can put your teeth in. And you can show him around a little."

"Good idea, Jean. Good idea." Bert turned to me. "Follow me, young man."

I followed him.

## Chapter 17

"You're not here for money are you?" Bert asked me as we walked.

"No, I'm not," I said.

"Here to sue me?"

"No. Should I be?" I asked him.

"Not if you'd ask me!" he said with a chuckle. "So why *are* you here?" he asked.

"Let's wait until we get to your room. Okay?" I asked him.

He shrugged his thin shoulders.

"Okay," he said. "I'm old. I'm patient. I can wait. But not too long. Ya hear? Because like I said. I'm *old*!"

He laughed again.

Was everybody in this place so cheerful?

We got to his room.

It was a nice room. Homey. Looked lived in. Comfortable.

"Nice place you have here," I said honestly.

"*I* like it," he said.

"So, Mr. Herpichio…" I started.

Before I could say more? He spoke.

"Hey. You said it right! Thanks! Most people say: her pih *chee* oo. With the accent on the third syllable. But they sound like they're sneezing. Don't you think? Her pih *chee* oo. God bless you."

The man laughed at his own joke.

I did too.

I started to ask him again. But before I could speak, he went on.

"I keep telling people! It's: her *peach* ee oo. Her *peach* ee oo! A nice Italian name."

"Yes it is," I told him.

"So what's your name?" he asked me.

"Dan. Dan Corbett," I replied.

"You're not Italian," he said.

"No. I'm not."

He waved his hand. "That's okay. Don't worry about it."

I wasn't worried about it.

"Let me just get my teeth in. Then we'll talk. Okay?" he asked.

"Okay," I said.

He was a feisty old guy!

He went to the dresser and picked up a set of teeth.

He shoved them in his mouth.

Then he clacked his teeth together. Once Twice Three times.

"Okay. I'm good now," he said.

He turned around and smiled.

"You look good with teeth," I told him.

He smiled wider. "Thanks!"

"So. Let me tell you why I'm here."

"I wish you *would*," he said with a chuckle. "I'm not getting any younger, you know!"

If he'd be *quiet*, I'd have a chance to *tell* him!

"I own a junkyard," I started to explain.

"Oh. That's nice," he said.

"Yes, Well, I have an old 1930 Ford Coupe in the yard."

"They were beautiful!" he said. "My friend Billy had one of them. Billy McCoy. Ever heard of him?"

"No," I said. "Anyway…"

"Billy wasn't Italian either," Bert said. "But that was okay. I liked him a lot. He was a good guy. Even if he wasn't Italian."

I could tell this was going to take a long time!

"Okay. That's great. Anyhow…" I started again.

"I miss Billy. Haven't thought of him in years! He died at the end of 1948. Wow. That's sixty years ago. Time flies when you're having fun. Doesn't it?"

I wouldn't know. I wasn't having fun. And I was getting a headache.

"Look. Bert. Focus. Tell me. What do you know about that 1930 Ford Coupe?"

"I *am* telling you!" He sounded annoyed.

## Chapter 18

Just then, my cell phone rang.

Great! Would this nightmare ever end?!

"Excuse me, please," I said to Bert.

"Go right ahead," he said. He waved his hand in the air. "I'm not going anywhere."

Yeah. Well. Apparently? Neither was I.

"Hello?" I said into the phone.

"Hey, Dan. It's me, Bubba. Look. I hate to tell you this. I really do."

"But you're going to tell me anyhow. Right?" I asked.

My head started pounding.

"I have to," he said.

"No you don't," I said back.

"Yes. I do," he said clearly.

I rolled my eyes. I rubbed my temples. "All right. What's up?"

"You've got another problem."

"*Now* what?!" I said with frustration.

"A customer came in while you were gone."

"So?" I asked.

"So, they wanted a door," he said.

"So?" I asked again. "Did you sell it to them?"

"I tried," Bubba said. "But when I took the door off? Some papers came out."

"So?" I asked.

"They were military plans. *Official* military plans," he explained.

I groaned and rolled my eyes. "Oh, no. Here we go again! That's going to have to wait until after I finish with this problem. Okay?"

Bubba laughed. "It's *your* junkyard, not mine!"

"Look, I've got to go," I told him. "I'll catch up with you when I get back home."

"Did you find out about the machine gun yet?" Bubba asked.

"I'm working on it!" I said. "But who knows?!"

I looked at Bert.

He was sitting there smiling at me.

"I'll let you know when I get back. Okay?" I asked Bubba.

"Yeah. Sure," Bubba replied.

He hung up. So did I.

"Problems?" Bert asked.

I shrugged. "What else is new?!"

"So. Back to that car," he said.

"Did you own one?" I asked. Maybe it was his.

"No. But like I told you. My friend Billy did."

"So how does that help?" I asked Bert.

"It's probably *his* car in your yard," Bert said simply.

"It was seized. By the police. Just a few days after it came off the assembly line," I told Bert.

Bert laughed. "Yup. That was Billy's car all right."

Okay. Now we were getting somewhere.

"You *sure* you don't know about Billy?" he asked again.

"Positive," I replied.

"Well, you need to hear *this* story!" Bert said with a hearty laugh.

"Might there be a *machine gun* in this tale?" I asked.

"You know? I almost forgot about that," he said with a belly laugh.

I nodded. "Go on. Please."

"You see, my friend Billy and his brother had a freight business. But times got tough. And they almost lost their business. You with me so far?"

I nodded.

"Good. Okay. So, they sold their business. And they went into a different *type* of business."

He looked at me to see if I was listening.

Of *course* I was listening! I had nothing else to do and nowhere else to go.

He had a captive audience in me.

"You heard of prohibition?" he asked me.

## Chapter 19

"Sure," I said.

"Well," he said. "That was a strange time. A strange time indeed."

"I'd imagine," I said.

"Yes, well. Billy and his brother needed money. Times were hard. So they decided to go into the rum-running business. You ever heard of that?" he asked me.

"Yes," I said. "A time or two."

"Well, Billy and his brother? They were great at rum running! They were both sailors, so they knew the seas. That helped them find the finest liquor. They brought it home, too. Here. To America."

"But wasn't that illegal?"

"Sure was," Bert said. "Prohibition went from 1920 until 1933. That was thirteen years of people having to sneak things. *Thirteen years*, Dan! That's a long time."

"Yes it is," I agreed.

"Billy was known for bringing the finest whiskey to America," Bert said.

"Hm. I didn't know that," I said.

"Ever hear of the expression 'the real McCoy'?" he asked me.

"I *have* heard of that. People sometimes say, 'This is the real McCoy' or 'That's the real McCoy.'"

"Right!" Bert said. "Well, my friend Bill? *He's* where that phrase came from! If someone doubted the quality of the bootlegged liquor? People would ask if it was 'the real McCoy.' Because Billy only got the best! He only smuggled in the very best the world had to offer!"

"That would do it," I said with a grin.

"Billy became a household name! He was

known for his fine liquors. His rye. His whiskey. His fine wines. His stuff was great. Excellent!" Bert said with a wink and a smile. "I partook a time or two, myself."

That made me smile. Bert was a real character.

"So how do you think his car ended up in *my* junkyard?" I asked.

"That's easy! He *lived* here in Florida. He'd made a *lot* of money smuggling in booze during Prohibition."

"Was he ever caught?" I asked.

"Oh yeah," Bert said smoothly. "Once. And it wasn't pretty. Let me tell you!"

"What happened?" I asked.

"Whenever the government got close? Billy would sail into international waters. He was such a good sailor? He always outran them. He really frustrated them!"

"I'll bet," I said.

"And boy were they angry that he made them look bad," Bert said.

"I can imagine," I said honestly.

"At the end of 1923? The coast guard had orders to capture Bill. Even if he was in international waters. That's how fed up they were with him!"

"So what happened?"

"Oh, they got him all right!" Bert said. "They placed a shell right off his hull!"

"Did it kill him?" I asked.

"No. No," Bert said. "They didn't kill him. But he got captured."

"So he went to trial?" I asked.

"Nah. He didn't want a whole long, drawn out thing. So he pleaded guilty. They *did* catch him red handed," Bert said with a wink.

"Did he go to jail?" I asked.

"Yup. For nine months. Somewhere up in New Jersey. But as soon as he was out? He came back down to Florida."

"Was he still a rum runner?" I asked.

"Nah. He got into Florida real estate after that."

"But what about the machine gun?" I wondered aloud.

## Chapter 20

"He'd made a lot of enemies. Not just the United States government. But also the mafia. His little business stepped on a *lot* of toes. I'm talking organized crime here," he said easily. "That's how we got to be friends."

I raised my eyebrows in question.

"Not that I was in the mafia or anything," he said with a wink. "At least not on record. But Billy was a good guy. I liked him. He served his time. Got out. And lived a clean life after that. But that didn't stop the police and the mob from harassing him."

"So that's why the police seized his car?" I asked.

"Sure is," Bert said with a chuckle. "But it didn't matter. Billy didn't care. He was living right and wouldn't let it bother him."

"And the machine gun in the back?" I asked.

"Ach. That!" Bert waved his hand at that. "Bill only had that so he could *say* he had it. So no one would bother him. He even *bought* it from the mob. Just so they'd know he had it."

That made Bert laugh.

"But Bill would never *use* it! Lord knows he wouldn't hurt a fly," Bert said.

Then he chuckled.

"Bill was a good businessman. And a good sailor. He had a *great* sense of humor!" Bert said.

"I guess he'd have to" I replied.

Bert thought about that. "You would've liked him," Bert said to me. "Everyone did."

I needed to find out about that machine gun.

"So that gun. It wasn't used for, ah, anything?" I asked.

"Nah," he said with a wave of his hand. "It had never even been fired."

"Never?" I asked. That seemed odd.

"Believe it or not? Never! I even told Bill I'd take him somewhere. To teach him how to use it. But he said no. He didn't want to know."

Bert cracked up with the memory.

He laughed so hard, his teeth fell out.

"Whoops. Sorry," he said as he scooped them up off his lap. "That happens sometimes."

He shoved them back into his mouth.

"Like I said. Before he started living a clean life? Billy ticked off some pretty important leaders of organized crime. He never *used* the gun. Just bought it for protection. To show that he'd *had* it."

Then he started laughing again.

"He didn't even have any *ammo* for it!" Bert explained.

That must be true. We didn't find any ammo in the car. Or in the machine gun.

The gun must've been hidden pretty well! If the police hadn't found it? And the car came to the yard with the gun still hidden? It *couldn't* have been in a place where Bill could have gotten to it easily.

Bert was most likely telling the truth.

It made sense. It fit with what we'd found. And with what the police *didn't* find!

"You said he died in 1948," I said.

"Yes. That's right," Bert replied.

"So is that how he died? He got hit by the mafia?" I asked.

I didn't know what I'd said that was so funny, but Bert thought it was hilarious.

"No. No. No," he said.

He was laughing so hard, I was afraid his teeth would fall out again.

"The *mafia* didn't get him! A grape did," Bert said.

He got killed by a *grape*?! What was I missing?

Was that an inside name for a job in the organized crime family?

You've got the "boss." The "soldiers." The "don."

And I knew there were a lot of other titles that I didn't know of.

But could they have… the "grapes"?

I didn't know. But it just didn't sound like it fit.

I couldn't picture any mafia guy trying to work his way up to being a "grape."

It seemed so… uncool.

I mean, really. I'd never heard anyone getting gunned down for not respecting the "grape."

"Go figure," Bert said. "With all the people out there who hated him? Looking to kill him? It was weird that Bill died by choking on a grape!"

Bert was no longer laughing. In fact, he now looked sad.

"He choked on a grape?" I asked.

"Yup. Choked on a grape and died. Had no one around to give him the Heimlich maneuver. That's why I live here. Lots of people around. When *I* die? It's *not* going to be because I choked on a grape!" Bert said with a grin. "I miss Bill a lot, though. He was a good guy."

Bill McCoy was quite the character!

But so was Bert Herpichio!

I'd have to visit him again sometime.

Now that Dan's solved *this* mystery,

read the next **JUNKYARD DAN** book,

**PLANS,**

to find out what those military plans were!

Are they top secret?

Did someone *use* those plans?

Were they from a war?

And if so…

which war were they from?

Find out by reading the *next* book in the series!

# Want to read more
# **JUNKYARD DAN**
# books?

Go online to
**www.NoxPress.com**
to see what's being released!

Books can easily be purchased online
or you can contact **Nox Press**
via the Website for quantity discounts.

### Are you a fan?
Do you want us to put *your* comments
up on our Website?
If so, please e-mail them to:
**NoxPress@gmail.com**

## NOX PRESS
**books for that extra kick to give you more power**

**www.NoxPress.com**